GIVING
GOD'S LOVE
To OTHERS

How To Show Christian Love Behavior

ARLETTE THOMAS FLETCHER

Giving God's Love To Others

How To Show Christian Love Behavior

ISBN: 978-0-9715510-7-7

DEDICATION

This book is dedicated to my mother Inez Rosebud Thomas. She understood unconditional love because she gave it to her children and anyone who needed help. She was a loving and giving human being who always put others before herself. It was this love that she showed me that helped me to take my journey toward the Lord Jesus Christ. It inspired me to want to learn more about God's love.

To my husband Kenneth, and my sons Charles and Joel: without your love and support this may have never been possible.

ACKNOWLEDGMENTS

I honor my Lord and Savior Jesus Christ who is the light of my life. I thank you, Lord, for all the patience and mercy that you have shown me in my life.

I am humbled by the unconditional love given to me and the forgiveness you have shown me in my imperfect state. I know that I am a sinner saved by the grace of God and not of anything I did, but by your grace and mercy. I am nothing without you breathing the breath of your word into my life every day.

Thank you for showing me that **"being a doer of the word and not a hearer only deceiving yourself"** must be my mantra in life. I praise God for the Lord Jesus Christ showing me that true love comes from the deepest parts of my soul.

Thank you, Lord, for teaching me that true Christian love behavior is consistently patient, enduring, faithful, and true to God first and then to itself. I hope to always look to God for guidance in all circumstances and believe that God will supply the answer through His Word.

TABLE OF CONTENTS

I Corinthians 13: 1-4

"Though I speak with the tongues of men and of angels, but have not love, I have become sounding brass or a clanging cymbal. ²And though I have the gift of prophecy, and understand all mysteries and all knowledge, and though I have all faith, so that I could remove mountains, but have not love, I am nothing. ³And though I bestow all my goods to feed the poor, and though I give my body to be burned, but have not love, it profits me nothing.

⁴Love suffers long and is kind; love does not envy; love does not parade itself, is not puffed up; ⁵ does not behave rudely, does not seek its own, is not provoked, thinks no evil; ⁶ does not rejoice in iniquity, but rejoices in the truth; ⁷ bears all things, believes all things, hopes all things, endures all things."

FOREWORD

My heart is bursting with so many powerful passages of LOVE scriptures, that I know Pastor Arlette will be sharing with you in this dynamic piece of work. There is one particular scripture that says it all and it speaks volumes. The scripture is found in I Corinthians 12:4-5. *"Love is patient, love is kind, it does not envy, it does not boast, it is not proud. It does not dishonor others, it is not self-seeking, it is not easily angered, it keeps no record of wrongs."*

This is what God desires us to do as we show Christian love, HIS love, towards each other, daily. Not just when you feel like it or when it is convenient, but it should follow us every single day, just as "Goodness and Mercy" follow us. It should not only follow us but also dwell within us just as Christ dwells in us richly!

I think that the Christian Community has gotten off track, in the area of displaying genuine Christian love behavior. It is time for us to go back to our first LOVE! Revelation 2:4, (NLT) says, *"But I have this complaint against you. You don't love me or each other as you did at first."*

We must not lose our focus and get distracted. There is so much going on in our World that will get you off the path! We must remember that "God is Love." Our first love. "We love because He first loved us." John 13:34 says "*A new command I give you; Love one another. As I have loved you, so you must love one another.*" In the pages of this amazing work, the author seeks to help you in so many ways, but her writings will lead you straight into the "LOVE ZONE."

I have known Arlette Thomas-Fletcher for 10+ years. I met Arlette at the Urban Playwrights United Conference, where I was one of the speakers. She stood out from the crowd. I saw her, I felt her heart and her spirit. **She is** a visionary. **She is** purpose driven. **She is** a giver. **She is** a true worshipper. **She is** passionate. **She is** forthright. **She is** humble.

She is bold. **She is** gifted. **She is** an encourager. **She is** wise. **She is** fierce. **She is** bold. **She is** a fighter. **She is** faithful. **She** is loving. **She** is caring. **She is** a Conqueror. **She is** courageous. **She is** determined. **She is** unapologetically BLACK. **She is** confident. **She is** fearless. **She is** a lover of life and mankind. She leaves no stone unturned.

Above all, she LOVES God with every fiber of her being. She has been chosen for such a time as this. **SHE IS** GOD'S proverbial woman of substance! All of who I say, **"She is,"** did not come overnight. She earned every single title. As you dig deep into her writings you will understand why her **"SHE IS....**" list is so long. I could have gone on and on, but it would have turned into a chapter.

The word of God says, "to much is given, much is required." Her struggles, her challenges, her ups and downs, her disappointments, her loses, her pain and all of those things that may have made her, at times, question God, she turned every scar into a star and continued to shine for the King of King and Lord of Lords. Those stumbling blocks did not stop her, they fueled her.

She 'GOT UP" with all power in her hands because she trusted God and leaned not to her own understanding. She pushed herself and made a quality decision to rise up and step out on faith knowing that HE who began a good work in her would be faithful to complete it. Arlette dressed herself in the whole armor of God and kept pressing towards the mark for the prize of the high calling which is in Christ Jesus.

She has no fears because she has the love of God driving her. *"There is no fear in love. But perfect love drives out fear."* I can't wait for you to dive into Arlette's toolbox. These tools have come from some of her past and present experiences while on her journey! She would tell you that she is still adding tools to her box because of the life-lessons that are never ending in our lives.

As she pulls out the various tools, via her writings, she will begin the rebuilding process on her readers. We all have areas that need to be rebuilt, reconstructed, renewed, renovated, restored, reignited, refreshed, and revived! When we trust God, we will grow and go through our struggles, as He wraps His loving arms around us and carries us through.

We see His hand of mercy and we say, "I am *wiser, I am strong, I am better, so much better,*" as Pastor Marvin Sapp pinned the lyrics and sang the song, *"Never Could Have Made It."* I invite you to grab a seat and open your heart, mind and soul to the words and nuggets that will be dropped into your spirit through the writings of Elder Arlette Thomas-Fletcher.

When she heard the call to write this book, she yielded and said YES. When she said YES, the Lord opened the flood gates of her heart and use her to speak life into those who desire to hear what the spirit of the Lord is saying.

As Arlette shares her stories with you, I am confident that you will be empowered, enlightened, elevated challenged, committed and convicted as the love of God overtakes you and launches you into His realm of a love like you have never experienced or encountered before. Get onboard, fasten your seatbelt, and enjoy the ride on this Holy Ghost Love Train!!!

DeEtta M. West

INTRODUCTION

With the current events that have happened in our world one may take pause in "Giving God's Love To Others." No one wants to show love to someone that comes at them with a weapon in hand. What God wants us to do is seek him when we are in pain. Sometimes that pain runs so deep that we think it will never stop hurting. But God is our healer and bandage for the wounds that we have suffered.

If you are unsure about how to begin to heal from past hurts and current situations and how to start to show love to others, then you need to read this book. This book will guide you through the Bible and how God helps us to know what showing Christian love to others means. I acknowledge that I may have been kind at times to individuals and not shown them the true love of God.

We often think that we have the right to lash out at people when they are cruel and mean to us. As the old parable says, "two wrongs don't make a right". If both people are fighting then who stops the fight? Someone has to have the humility to forgive and to mediate to diffuse an explosive situation.

Violence is not the answer to any situation. However, we often feel like displaying acts of violence because we are angry and furious with those who harm us. Sometimes we put up with people until they push our buttons and set us off. But, if we learn what showing God's love really means we will be able to learn how to diffuse situations and seek God for peace.

I understand that some things may seem like they are so horrid that you may want to do things that you should not do. But, don't do those things, just seek God first. The Bible teaches us that "vengeance is mine sayeth the Lord." No one is perfect we are all human. I am human too, but I am also a Christian and that is why I can speak about the difference in being tolerant of someone and truly showing the love of God.

I learned that showing Christian love to others is very important to the Lord. In the Bible it says in **1 John 4:20 KJV "If a man say, I love God, and hateth his brother, he is a liar: for he that loveth not his brother whom he hath seen, how can he love God whom he hath not seen?"** Sometimes we all put up with people and are kind to them but in our hearts, we don't really have any love for them.

We are only being cordial and respectful because we have to, or because they oversee us. A suitable example of this would be an employer, boss, or even a person who is teaching us in school. This is something I believe I did before I understood what showing God's love to others really meant. It was not intentional, it was only because I did not know the difference between showing the love of God and kindness.

The world defines love as being good and nice to people who are good and nice to you. The world expects that you must work hard to qualify for love. However, the opposite is true in the Kingdom of God. We did not do anything to qualify for God giving us His only begotten son to die for our sins. It was a gift that we paid nothing for.

The Bible says, **"But God demonstrates His own love toward us, in that while we were still sinners, Christ died for us"** (Romans 5:8 NKJV) Having received this great love from God, we are expected to show the same to people in our everyday lives, even when they are undeserving of such love. When I was a child I remember being teased by children at school and sometimes being bullied.

I felt very betrayed and hurt because I had not done anything to deserve what happened to me. So many of us have suffered the same kind of hurt in school and at work by people bullying us and sometimes terrorizing our reputation, making you feel like, "why is this happening to me"? Why would someone who doesn't even know you just attack you or your reputation?

I found out later in life it was because these people did not know how to show love. Many times, they hurt others because they had been hurt in their own lives. So, pain begets pain. As you read this book you will find that this happened to Joseph with his brothers. We go through and explain this and how God took him on a journey that lead to healing for him and his family.

Our world needs to understand the importance of giving God's love to others. This book helps you look at circumstances that may be similar to what you have gone through in your own life. It also leads you through the Bible so that you can see that some of these things have happened to others and how God helped them through and showed them how to heal.

I will be talking about Christian love Behavior, how to learn love behavior, showing it in your actions, and teaching others how to show it. My prayer is that all of the truth that God will reveal in this book will impact your life, family, church and community for greater fruitfulness in Jesus name. My purpose for writing How To Show Christian love behavior is to encourage those who are discouraged because they don't understand why the people around them are not extending the love of God to them in the way that it should be given.

When I was a young Christian, I was injured so many times in the church, but it was God that showed me through His word that many did not know how to show the love of God. That is why I wrote this book. It is to be a support to help people to know that God wants us to receive and give love to one another in a kind and unconditional manner.

That as Christians we are to live a life that is committed to the work of the Lord Jesus Christ. Understanding that we are to hold him up as our example for giving love to one another with the understanding that he loved us no matter what and stood by us through all our life journeys.

We know that the devil wants us to look at what others do and sometimes be affected by the damage that is done to us. But we must look to the Lord and commit to loving our neighbor as ourselves and forgiving one another. Understanding that we must pray without ceasing for God's grace to carry us through our many trials and tribulations.

The love of God is what has kept me all my life and it is what helps me through all of life's mishaps and situations. Without God I would be lost in a dark fog of life without a light to guide my way. God is truly love. If we are willing to let him show us his love, we will understand what Christian love behavior is and how to show it to one another.

WHAT IS CHRISTIAN LOVE BEHAVIOR?

Johnhain graphic artist

The Merriam-Webster dictionary defines love as "strong affection for another arising out of kinship or personal ties." While it is not my intention to go into all the different types of love, I think it is important to touch on them so that we can understand what Christian love behavior means.

There are four types of love.

Eros Love: which is known as "erotic love." This love is based on a deep sensual feeling toward another person.

Philos Love: This is a love that is found in a friendship between two people.

Storge Love: this is a love that is shown between a mother and son or a brother and a sister. It is the kind of love that exists between family members and friends and even spouses.

Agape Love: This is unconditional love and that is the love that we are talking about showing when we speak of Christian love behavior. Agape love is the love that God himself shows to us. It is a love that we did nothing to earn and has no conditions. There are no strings attached. ***"For God so loved the world that he gave his only begotten Son that we might have eternal life."* (John 3:16)**

"He who does not love does not know God, for God is love." **(1 John 4:8)** The scripture teaches us that God does not just love us, but He is love. Christian love behavior is the act of showing the love that God has imparted to us from the Holy Spirit. This love that is shown to others and not just spoken of throughout the Bible is displayed in the actions of our savior the Lord Jesus Christ.

He ministered to people while He walked on the earth. We see a demonstration of this love when Jesus was crucified at Calvary and said to the Father in **Luke 23:34** *"Then Jesus said, "Father forgive them, for they do not know what they do"*. As His life was being sacrificed for our sins, He looked at our filth, sin, and heartlessness. He forgave and loved mankind through the pain of the crucifixion.

God is not asking you to hang on a cross, but He is asking you to give your life to Him, to commit your heart to show the love of God to all men, which requires the action of showing love through your behavior toward other human beings. What God expects from us in Christian love behavior is to show the same kind of unconditional love that He has bestowed on us to our fellow human beings.

He wants us to show this with our actions not just in words alone.

Central Truth: There are different types of love, but the Agape love which God demonstrated to us is true love. That is the type that God expects us to show to others.

LEARNING CHRISTIAN
LOVE BEHAVIOR

Bella87 graphic artist

Christian love behavior is something that I am still growing in and learning every day. Christian love behavior does not come to us by default, we have to learn it. I learned that it is important to understand the difference between just being nice and showing love and kindness to another individual. These lessons were learned over more than twenty years of me receiving love from the people of God.

As Christians, we need to understand that God is calling us to have the heart of a servant which requires us to be open to all people. While we may think that we are open to all people sometimes we are not, and this shows through our actions and behavior. The way we treat others during those times when we are put in uncomfortable positions shows how we must humble ourselves and allow God to show us what to do when things are difficult.

We must pray for guidance, so we don't miss being a blessing to those whom the Lord has sent us to help. I know there were people who needed to receive the love of God from the people of God, but they were misunderstood. These individuals were homeless, drug addicted, and in some cases criminals who were broken down and ready to receive God's love.

But, because the people who were in the position to help them could not see what God was doing they were not able to help them come to a place of deliverance. Other times, I watched as others who showed the love of God were injured and hurt by people who had been through much pain and hurt, such that they did not know how to show God's love to others. So, they hurt the very people who were trying to help them and love them through their painful situations.

I have experienced much of God's love from the people of God, but the greatest love I have ever experienced is God's love. God's love is unconditional, and He takes time to teach you things that no one else will do. God taught me that when He saved me, He saved me just as I was. He accepted me the way I was. Yes, I had repented of my sins, confessed my sins, and accepted Jesus as my Lord and Savior.

I was baptized in water and received the Holy Spirit but the old man, which was to die, was dying. I thought that the old man died when I came to Christ. No, Paul said, "*I die daily*," and if Paul had to die daily then what was he dying to? Sin! That was when I realized that if God saved me and I had low self-esteem, then that was what I brought to Him when He saved me.

If I had a quick temper, then that was also something I brought with me. If I was a fornicator that was also something I brought with me. That was why He said I should cast my cares upon Him. I had been forgiven of my sins and the grace of the Lord Jesus Christ covered me. But I was a sinner saved by the grace of God through the shed blood of the Lord Jesus Christ. I had to grow in that grace through which I was saved.

As I grew, I was delivered from old sins based on my desire to be delivered and my faith in God. The Bible says, *"If we ask anything in His name, believing it, we will receive"* (**Matthew 21:22**) If we have not learned who God is, how can we believe in His Word? If we have not learned that God is love, how can we believe in His word that says we should love one another? This requires being taught what living a Christian life means.

It doesn't matter what age we are when we come to the Lord. The Bible teaches us that when we come to Christ we come as babes. **1 Peter 2:2 ² "As newborn babes, desire the sincere milk of the word, that ye may grow thereby:"** We are babes who have to learn how to behave according to the principles of the Kingdom of God. I learned that I had to die to the old man daily for fifteen years.

Before God came into my life, I knew a life of only flesh and some religious activities such as church on Sundays, but no real Christian life. God showed me that I had to be renewed by the Word of God and that I had to live a Godly life, but this was not something that I learned overnight. This is the reason the Apostle Peter admonished us that we should desire the sincere milk of the word of God so that we can grow by it. **(1 Peter 2:2)**

The day that I was saved is the day that my life changed, my heart changed, and I was a new creature in Christ, but I still lived in this flesh. I had to grow day by day to become the kind of person God wanted me to be. So Godly behavior was being taught to me day by day by God through the Word of God. If I did not learn and read by going to Sunday School, attending Bible Class, reading, and studying on my own, how would I have learned what God's love meant?

This is not something that you know the moment you are saved. God's love behavior is a lifestyle we must learn because it is strange to the old man's nature that we carry. Sure, you know how it feels to be loved by God. You know the difference between how you felt and what you used to feel from the "love" the world called love.

But, do you know how to always behave in love? Do you know how to show Christian love behavior? I did not know how to show it although I was genuinely a nice person, so I knew how to be nice to people. But Christian love behavior requires more than being nice to people. It requires showing kindness, compassion, and understanding. Sometimes your flesh is tired or irritated and does not want to show these elements of human tenderness.

With the love of God, you will learn and understand how love behavior teaches you that it is through the love of Christ that people are drawn to Him. So, if we don't show love behavior, how do we know we are showing love? The love of God has a pattern of behavior and expression. We learn these patterns and expressions from God Himself who is love. If we have not known the love of God and understood His behavior and expression, we cannot show love behavior to others.

During the last meal with the disciples, Jesus issued a new commandment "love one another". In **John 13:35** the scripture references the importance of men knowing us as the disciples of Christ by the love that we show to each other and others. [35]" **By this shall all men know that ye are my disciples, if ye have love one to another."**

Jesus wanted us to show love as He did to all people. He was not just being nice but genuinely giving of his heart and Himself in service to those that needed Him. Remember, there is a difference between love behavior and being nice. The world can be nice one minute and mean the next, but love behavior is always kind. Remember when Jesus turned over the tables of the moneychangers in the temple, do you think He was showing love? I do.

Why do I think He was showing love? Jesus saw the money changers and the seats of them that sold doves in the temple. He said in the scripture in **Matthew 21:12 13"And said unto them, It is written, My house shall be called the house of prayer; but ye have made it a den of thieves**." Then Jesus healed the blind and the lame that came to Him.

While He was firm with the money changers because of their wrongdoing he still showed them the love as a father to an undisciplined child. It's because love can be firm when we need to be shown right from wrong. You know sometimes you have to discipline your children, but never for a moment do you stop loving them in the process of showing them discipline.

Love behavior is important; it stops us from being cruel, and unkind, and showing worldly harshness to people around us. No one is perfect but Jesus Himself. We are still striving to grow toward the love that God wants us to show to one another.

In the Bible, it says, *"How can you say you love God whom you cannot see when you do not love your brother who you see every day?"* **1 John 4:20**. God wants us to show love and He has taken the time in His Word to show us how to show love behavior.

Central Truth: Love behavior is the spirit of God working in us through a pattern of consistent kindness, compassion, and patience we learn from God and show to others even when they are undeserving. We are expected to be groomed in this loving behavior and grow in it day by day as we learn more about God.

OBSTACLES TO SHOWING CHRISTIAN LOVE BEHAVIOR

by Anja from Pixabay

Love behavior is not the human side of us that onlyreacts nicely when others are nice. Every child of God desires to be like God. Showing the love of God through our actions is the only way we can reflect on what He has taught us. The Bible teaches us to be doers of the word and not hearers only deceiving ourselves.

The scripture tells us in **Matthew 5:1313"Ye are the salt of the earth: but if the salt have lost his savour, wherewith shall it be salted? it is thenceforth good for nothing, but to be cast out, and to be trodden under foot of men."** It further tells in **Matthew 5:14-16¹⁴ "Ye are the light of the world. A city that is set on an hill cannot be hid. ¹⁵ Neither do men light a candle, and put it under a bushel, but on a candlestick; and it giveth light unto all that are in the house. ¹⁶ Let your light so shine before men, that they may see your good works, and glorify your Father which is in heaven."**

That is the only way we can be as light and salt in this world. The only way we can attract the world to the Lord is by showing Christian love behavior among ourselves as children of God and to everyone we come across in our daily lives.

However, some habits, incidents, and situations present obstacles to our desire to show Christian love behavior toward others. We must carefully screen and uproot these habits and attitudes from our lives if we sincerely desire to show God's love to others.

These habits and attitudes are entrenched in the pattern of behavior of the old nature that we were used to before we came to the Lord. We must not yield to them anymore now that we have come to the knowledge of the truth.

Examples of such behaviors are shown below.

The War of the Flesh and the Spirit

Jose the storyteller

II Corinthians 10:3-5 "For though we walk in the flesh, we do not war after the flesh: 4 For the weapons of our warfare are not carnal, but mighty through God to the pulling down of stronghold; 5 Casting down imaginations, and every high thing that exalteth itself against the knowledge of God, and bringing into captivity every thought to the obedience of Christ; 6 And having a readiness to revenge all disobedience, when your obedience is fulfilled."

I have explained earlier that there was an old man that controlled our lives before we came to Christ. This old man is the carnal nature of man. When we come to Jesus, God input His very nature into us, so that we can reflect His character. It is the new nature of God that testifies to the fact of the salvation that has taken place in us. However, we are babes in the Lord. We are just learning the new way of life in the nature of God.

The old man in us struggles with the new nature of God. We become strong to reflect the new nature as we consistently resist the old man and yield to the new nature of God in us. *"For the flesh lusts against the Spirit, and the Spirit against the flesh; and these are contrary to one another, so that you do not do the things that you wish."* (Galatians 5:17 NKJV)

This war is the reason some Christians find themselves behaving in ways that are contrary to God's love. Therefore, we must grow by consistently yielding to the Spirit of the Lord through the word of God instead of giving in to the dictates of the flesh.

Lack of Self-control

Free-Photos

Luke 21:19 "In your patience possess ye your souls"

When driving cars in traffic, people have been known to get frustrated, yell, and shout at other drivers. In New York City, there was one occurrence where a driver shot another driver for cutting him off in traffic. It is important not to allow the circumstances that surround us to affect us in such a way that causes us to harm others. Life is full of unexpected turns and twists.

So many times, things don't happen as we plan, and we get frustrated. However, as Christians who are learning how to show love, we must exercise self-control. We must learn how to conquer our emotions and put them in check. If we must act in love, then we must learn not to release our negative emotions on others. Uncontrolled emotions will make us harm others with or without the intention to do so.

Confused Minds

Rama Krishna Karumanchi

Proverbs 3:5-6 "Trust in the Lord with all thine heart; and lean not unto thine own understanding. 6 In all thy ways acknowledge him, and he shall direct thy paths."

In life, there are so many choices to make, and many people don't know which road to choose. We are confronted daily with choices and many decisions that may lead to confusion.

A confused mind cannot act appropriately. Instead of allowing choices and decisions to confuse our minds, we should learn to turn to God for guidance, counsel, and direction at all times. He is never tired of providing guidance and direction to us.

He says in His Word, *"If anyone of you lacks wisdom, let him ask of God, that giveth to all men liberally, and upbraideth not and it shall be given him"* (**James 1:5**) When your mind is clear and at peace, you will automatically seek to be at peace with others which is another way of showing love.

Anxiety

Mohamed_Hassan graphic artist

Philippians 4:6 "Be anxious for nothing but in everything through prayer and supplication make your request known to God."

Sometimes the stress of dealing with so many things at once overwhelms you because you do not know if you will complete the task given to you in the time outlined. In the race to meet deadlines, we shove and push at others, sometimes without the intention to hurt them. Sometimes, we are so caught up in the rush to finish our tasks that we miss the opportunity to show God's love. We must learn to cast all our cares on God.

Anger

Ashish_Choudhary graphic artist

Ephesians 4:26 "Be ye angry, and sin not: let not the sun go down upon your wrath."

A lot of times when we are frustrated or irritated our first reaction is anger, but I am learning that it is possible to express displeasure or disappointment without giving in to anger. Anger is one of the tools the devil uses to interfere in our life and relationship. A lot of damage can be done to others and ourselves in a short moment of anger.

Anger Leads To Rage

Openclipart-Vector source

"Be angry, and do not sin; do not let the sun go down on your wrath, nor give place to the devil"
Ephesians 4:26-27

Have you ever been so frustrated with learning new things like computers that you felt like you could become violent?

Rage is a dangerous and explosive emotion that the devil wants your anger to reach through unbearable violent frustration. It is often short-lived but highly destructive. Rage is when we allow a little fire to become an inferno. The best antidote is to quench the anger as soon as it rises.

Jealousy Damages Relationships

Timisu graphic artist

In our world, there are people at different levels of success with different levels of talents and gifts. Some people can achieve the success which allows them to be extremely successful in ministry, business, sports, entertainment, and many other fields. We know some of these people to be Bill Gates, Steve Jobs, Kobe Bryant, Earvin "Magic" Johnson, Michael B. Jordan, Viola Davis, Robert De Niro, Meryl Streep, and many others.

Sometimes we look at these individuals with admiration. Some people look at them with resentment and jealousy. As we grow up we are surrounded by so many talented people. **When we go to school when we are children, we join sports teams, and we compete against someone that may have greater skill than we do.** When we run a race against them, and they win sometimes we find ourselves being a good sport and congratulating them.

Other times we might resent them for beating us at something we wanted to win. We are all born with gifts and talents that God has given each of us. Some of us work hard on our talents and become superstar athletes, artists, vocalists, businesspeople, and geniuses in aeronautical engineering, physics, and other fields. We all have something special to contribute to the world.

So why do we resent others when they have a gift or ability that seems more interesting or better than ours? We see jealousy rearing its ugly face so often. In families, this is what our parents used to call sibling rivalry. It is not a good thing when you envy or resent your brother or sister because they are better at something than you are.

They are your family, and you should always be excited about their achievements because their achievements are the families' accomplishments. When we look in the Bible we see in **Genesis 37:3-11[3] "Now Israel loved Joseph more than all his children, because he was the son of his old age: and he made him a coat of many colours.[4] And when his brethren saw that their father loved him more than all his brethren, they hated him, and could not speak peaceably unto him.**

[5] And Joseph dreamed a dream, and he told it his brethren: and they hated him yet the more.[6] And he said unto them, Hear, I pray you, this dream which I have dreamed:[7] For, behold, we were binding sheaves in the field, and, lo, my sheaf arose, and also stood upright; and, behold, your sheaves stood round about, and made obeisance to my sheaf.

[8] And his brethren said to him, Shalt thou indeed reign over us? or shalt thou indeed have dominion over us? And they hated him yet the more for his dreams, and for his words.

⁹ And he dreamed yet another dream, and told it his brethren, and said, Behold, I have dreamed a dream more; and, behold, the sun and the moon and the eleven stars made obeisance to me. ¹⁰ And he told it to his father, and to his brethren: and his father rebuked him, and said unto him, What is this dream that thou hast dreamed? Shall I and thy mother and thy brethren indeed come to bow down ourselves to thee to the earth?¹¹ And his brethren envied him; but his father observed the saying."

It is a story of a young man who was born to his father in his old age. A young man whom his father loved so much that he made him a coat of many colors. That young man was Joseph. One day Joseph had a dream and he told it to his father, mother, and brothers. In the dream there were sheaves and Joseph's sheaf was above his father's, mother's, and brother's sheaves.

Their sheaves bowed down to his sheaves. Joseph did not know what the dream meant when he told it to his father. He only knew he dreamt it. His father and brothers took offense to the dream and asked him does this mean that they would bow down to him and that he would rule over them.

Joseph was only innocently telling them a dream that God had given him. Later, Joseph's father told him to go and find his brothers. His brothers now harboring jealousy and resentment in their hearts toward Joseph were plotting to harm him and even kill him. All of this is malice because a young man was loved by his father, given a coat of many colors, and had a dream that he shared.

I am sure his brothers had their own abilities and their father loved them as well. It was not enough. They looked at Joseph and what he had and began to lust after his coat and his dream. Joseph approached them, and one of them said **"this dreamer cometh."** First, they plotted to kill him, and later they dropped him in a pit and sold him off to the Midianites. Why did they do this?

Because they were jealous and resented their own flesh and blood. Joseph was their brother and their younger brother at that. Jealousy is one of the most malicious things that happen in our world. It has divided more family relationships than can be numbered. God does not want us to be jealous of one another. He wants us to love one another.

The Bible says **1John 4:20** [20] **"If a man say, I love God, and hateth his brother, he is a liar: for he that loveth not his brother whom he hath seen, how can he love God whom he hath not seen?"** How can you love God whom you have not seen when you can't love your very own brother or sister whom you see every day?

There is no reason to ever be jealous, envious, or resentful of anyone. We were all given gifts and abilities by God. Embrace your gift and your ability. Stop looking at what someone else has and realize who you are and how special you are in this world and what wonderful things you can offer to mankind.

When you accept Christ into your heart you will find that God gives us access to spiritual gifts that can serve the church in many ways. These gifts are in the areas of administration, being an apostle, discernment, evangelism, exhortation, faith, giving, healing, helps, hospitality, knowledge, leadership, mercy, prophecy, serving, speaking in tongues, teaching, and wisdom.

Hypocritical Behavior

Sammy-Sander graphic artist

Merriam-Webster's definition of a hypocrite is a person who puts on a false appearance of virtue or religion. God loves all of us unconditionally and Jesus was a true example of God's truth, honesty, and love. He lived a life of service to all mankind. He showed us the importance of allowing the works we do to speak for us. The Bible teaches us to be a doer of the word not a hearer only deceiving ourselves.

James 1:22-24 **²² "But be ye doers of the word, and not hearers only, deceiving your own selves. ²³ For if any be a hearer of the word, and not a doer, he is like unto a man beholding his natural face in a glass: ²⁴ For he beholdeth himself, and goeth his way, and straightway forgetteth what manner of man he was."**

Many churchgoers read the Bible and can quote scripture, but our lives do not reflect any of the things that we have learned in the word of God. The Bible says that the Lord would rather we be hot or cold or he will spew us out of his mouth. The Lord does not approve of a lukewarm Christian.

Some people profess to have moral values, but their lives don't reflect the standards that they claim they believe in. Hypocritical behavior is a behavior where you wear two faces or live two lifestyles. It is a behavior that shows that we are not sincere in our convictions. The most disappointing thing is when someone is living a false life and professing to have a heart for God. God knows each of our hearts.

Luke 20:46-47 says [46] **"Beware of the scribes, which desire to walk in long robes, and love greetings in the markets, and the highest seats in the synagogues, and the chief rooms at feasts;** [47] **Which devour widows' houses, and for a shew make long prayers: the same shall receive greater damnation."** He knows when we are sincere. Hypocritical behavior is not a behavior where we are just falling short in our Christian walk.

This is a behavior where the person knows that they are not living a Godly life and they continue doing it on purpose. Many times, people who show hypocritical behavior try to take the light of truth off themselves by shining a false light on another person. So many of us are very judgmental determining that someone is wrong without even understanding the person or their circumstances.

We should always pray for God's guidance before we let our hearts believe the worse about another human being. So often we offend and injure someone because of what someone else says about the person without even knowing whether it is true or not. Often division happens in marriages, families, businesses, and churches due to individuals who proclaim to be Christians but display no real love behavior in their lives.

Many of these individuals cause much pain and heartache with their malice and divided spirit. These individuals need to go back to the Lord and repent and seek God for a renewal of their spirit and mind. The Bible teaches us that we should love everyone. It is hard when we encounter people who are hypocrites because they come packaged as Christian and then we find ourselves damaged by the harm they have done.

Deliverance from this behavior requires much fasting and prayer to destroy this spirit of hypocrisy. The fasting has to be done in the sincerity of your heart. Seeking God to deliver you from this behavior requires you to be true and honest with yourself. Our God can set us free from anything we need help with, we only have to ask him.

James 1:25-27 25 "But whoso looketh into the perfect law of liberty, and continueth therein, he being not a forgetful hearer, but a doer of the work, this man shall be blessed in his deed. 26 If any man among you seem to be religious, and bridleth not his tongue, but deceiveth his own heart, this man's religion is vain. 27 Pure religion and undefiled before God and the Father is this, To visit the fatherless and widows in their affliction, and to keep himself unspotted from the world."

When we are sincere about following God's purpose for our lives we are willing to humble ourselves to His will. It is so important to have the heart of a servant and be open to doing the things that will make a difference in those that are less fortunate than we are.

We should be able to commit our time and energy to helping in whatever capacity is needed.

Central Truth: We must get rid of anger, rage, lack of self-control, and carnality if we want to show Christian love behavior. These will always sabotage our efforts to draw the world to Christ.

ACTING IN LOVE

5540867 source

Love is an action word that means that we have to be intentional and purposeful in showing the love that we feel for another. Therefore, just saying you love someone does not mean you have exhibited Christian love behavior. Love behavior requires work, commitment, and sweat equity. If we are serious about conveying love behavior we must be committed to doing it.

It cannot be executed by default and we cannot assume that we are displaying love when there is no expression of giving charity to another human being. We must be deliberate about showing love behavior so that others can benefit from God's love moving through us to those around us. Love has characteristics that have been portrayed through the love Jesus showed in His ministry.

Jesus demonstrated His love for us on Calvary. **John 3:16 [16] "For God so loved the world, that he gave his only begotten Son, that whosoever believeth in him should not perish, but have everlasting life."** He didn't love us in words alone, He showed it. He had compassion for the hungry multitude and gave them food. He showed love to the woman caught in adultery and forgave her.

Matthew 14:17-20 [17] **"And they said unto Him, We have here but five loaves and two fishes.** [18] **And He said, Bring them hither to Me.** [19] **And He commanded the multitude to sit down on the grass, and took the five loaves and the two fishes; and looking up to Heaven, He blessed and broke the loaves and gave them to His disciples, and the disciples to the multitude.** [20] **And they all ate and were filled. And they took up the fragments that remained, twelve baskets full."** Everything He did was done in love.

Therefore, He has set an example for us to follow. There are deliberate actions we must take to show the love of God to others. These actions are not just to be shown to people we know, we must endeavor to promote them wherever we find ourselves, whether in our families, workplace, church, or society at large. Some of the examples of characteristics of love are explained in the pages that follow.

Giving

Image by Jeff Jacobs

John 3:16, "For God so love the world that He gave His only begotten son ...."

Giving is an attribute of God. He showed His love for us by sacrificing his son's life. He teaches us throughout the Bible that we should help others. The best form of giving is assisting people who cannot reciprocate. Give to the poor and the needy even if they are strangers. This show of love is not giving out of your abundance alone, sometimes it means offering your all or giving unselfishly. Giving unconditionally is an expression of Godly love.

Forgive

Image by Bente Boe

1 Peter 48, "And above all things have fervent love for one another, for love will cover a multitude of sins" (NKJV)

Forgiveness is to offer a pardon for an offense committed against you without any intention of revenge or ill feelings. To forgive is to allow an offense to pass without holding any grudge against the offender. As Christians, we must always have the willingness and readiness to forgive. The Bible encourages us to make allowance for each other's faults. We cannot claim to show Christian love behavior when we cannot forgive those that offend us in our families, workplace, church, or society. We must always be ready to forgive without being asked. We don't have to wait until someone apologizes before we forgive. Forgiveness should be a gift that we offer everyone, regardless of the offense.

Help the Elderly and the Vulnerable

Mohamed Hassan graphic artist

Romans 15:1, "We then who are strong ought to bear with the scruples of the weak and not to please ourselves"

We will always have people around us who are weak, either by the reason of age, illness, or trauma. We will meet them in our everyday life. We must help them in whatever way we can. You can help an elderly person cross the road or give them your seat on the bus. So often we look past the elderly and forget that they were the ones who built our world. They were the founders of everything that we can utilize in our everyday life. Now that they are older and vulnerable it is our time to serve them through the services that they need.

They may need us to bring food, cut their lawn, or even help them with putting on their clothes. We mustn't forget them in their time of need. They may need a visitor at the nursing home or hospital to comfort and assure them that everything will be all right. If you are blessed to live long enough someday someone will help you when you are in a vulnerable elderly state.

Don't forget about those with disabilities, they are vulnerable too. They are the ones who need support systems to help them have a normal life. They contribute and are a part of society at large. Sometimes their disability precludes them from working without assistance, but they are still able to contribute.

Disabilities come in so many different categories and levels of emotional and physical wellness. Every person that is disabled has a life that they are trying to live in our world to the best of their ability. They just need us to respect them and meet them where they need help when they need it.

Be Warm and Friendly

Utility_Inc Source

Proverb 18:24: "A man who has friends must himself be friendly"

Sometimes when people talk to us at work, home, school, or church environments, they make us feel as if we are on the hot seat. Often, people don't realize how nervous and uncomfortable they make others feel. Many times, we lose the opportunity to draw people to Jesus because of the unfriendly attitude we display.

Jesus rebuked the disciples for hindering the children from coming to Him. The Bible documented that Jesus cared for the children, laid hands on them, and prayed for them. Jesus was warm and had a welcoming attitude, which was the reason the multitude followed Him. We must learn the behavior of warmth and friendliness.

Be Patient With the Wounded

Serena Wong graphic artist

Proverbs 18:14 "The spirit of a man will sustain his infirmity, but a wounded spirit who can bear?"

Sometimes the people who need healing have multiple wounds and need more than one procedure done to get them stabilized. The person may need counseling or for us to take time out to give them special love and attention. They may just need a hug or for you to hold their hand.

Often it is expected that some individuals should have improved with the type of care and attention devoted to them. When an exhaustive amount of love and prayer has been invested into their life and there seems to be no change people may feel like they have no hope for deliverance.

It may get frustrating if they don't show improvement. However, we should not be impatient with them. Some individuals have suffered such a deep trauma in life that it is unbearable, and they see no healing for their circumstances. It may take a longer period to recover and open their hearts to God's healing power. We should not be infuriated. We must remember that God never stops helping us no matter how long it takes.

Let God Guide You

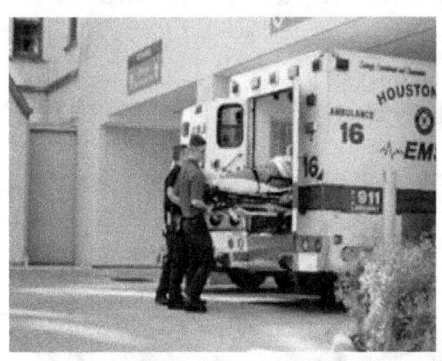

Artistoperations Source

Proverbs 18:13 "He that answereth a matter before he heareth it, it is folly and shame unto him."

If God has not called you to treat a wound, then you can do more damage than good in your efforts. When you try to diagnose or analyze the situation it can prove to be harmful.

This is because the person may need professional counseling or guidance from the clergy. Many Christians are guilty of this. We can hurt more than help when we do not allow God to direct our actions in our attempt to show love. Especially when we are dealing with a person who needs more than just our advice.

An untrained person trying to handle an accident victim may do more harm than good because he doesn't know what to do. In showing Christian love behavior, let us be guided by the Holy Spirit. He knows the deepest desire

Don't Gloat Over Those In Pain

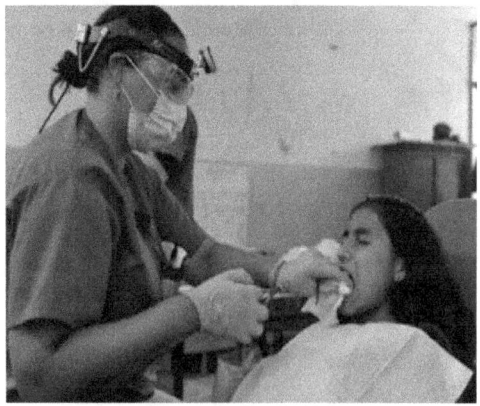

Image by David Mark

Psalm 109:22 "For I am poor and needy, and my heart is wounded within me."

When you are already suffering and in pain, you do not need anyone else to add to your hurt. We must not trample on those who are already down. One of the most common gloating I see, even in the church, is people making negative statements like **"I told you so"**, **"there they go again"**, **and "they are a waste of time"**.

When people are in pain, whether self-inflicted or otherwise, we should not add to the hurt by making insensitive comments or careless taunts. We should show empathy to those in pain, even if the pain has been caused by their carelessness.

Pray for others

Prawny/3436 source

James 5:16, "Confess your trespasses to one another, and pray for one another, that you may be healed. The effective, fervent prayer of a righteous man avails much."

Jesus is seated at the right hand of the Father and makes intercession for us. This is an example that we must pray for everyone. We must express Christian love to others by praying for them. Be concerned enough about the situation of others to present them to the Father. It is the duty of love to pray. Our prayer life should not be centered on ourselves. If Christ is praying for us we must extend that same love to the world.

Central Truth: Love is an action word that is expressed through actions. We must learn from the example of the Lord that we must act in love for everyone. We cannot love by words alone.

THE CHURCH: A SANCTUARY

12019 Source

The church is a congregation of the children of God. It is the Household of God where all the people who were ransomed by the shed blood of the Lamb belong. It is the gathering together of those who have come to the Lord from the world. The people in the church are supposed to have been redeemed from all sins, but we must not forget that they were taken from the world.

Everyone in the church once belonged to the world. The world is a place of different afflictions and scars, violence, war, abuse, divorce, betrayal, and other vices. Many people are already wounded and hurt by the world and unfortunately, they come to the church with that hurt and express the same to others. Others come to the church expecting to be healed and find rest from their troubles, but they encounter the same hurts that they have experienced in the world.

We must always be conscious of this fact. The church is full of people who were hurt by the world, people who are still growing in the understanding of Christian love behavior, and those who may still display some worldly traits.We must all be committed to learning and expressing Christian love behavior.

53

HOW TO MEDIATE BY EXAMPLE AND CREATE BETTER CHRISTIAN SOCIAL ENVIRONMENTS

Mote Oo source

I Timothy 2:5 "For there is one God, and one mediator between God and men, the man Christ Jesus ..."

Acting in love is learning how to ensure that peace reigns among the members of the church. We have established that the church is full of people who may have been wounded by the illnesses of the world. People may take out their pains on other people. God expects that we should learn how to meditate with the actions of love to establish a peaceful and warm environment in the church. It is only in the atmosphere of love and warmth that people can be healed and helped.

The Unintentional Evil

Public domain pictures source

"But the tongue can no man tame; it is an unruly evil, full of deadly poison." James 3:8

Many times, when we hurt someone, we have no clue as to what we have done. It also teaches us that we have a responsibility in the areas we are strong in to bear the weakness of our brothers and sisters. Sometimes we think that we are always strong in specific areas and then when we show weakness, we refuse to accept it.

We tell ourselves that this is the area that I am strong in and I should not mess up in this area. The scripture in **Romans 15:1-4** explains that during those times that we are strong, we can bear the burden of someone who is weak, but during those times that we are weak, the weak can bear our burdens because now they are strong.

One example of this may be that there are times when we lose our patience with a situation, circumstance, or person and we react in a way that is not Godly. This happens many times in the workplace, church, entertainment, and educational environment. Many times, however, when it happens a person may not want to admit that they could have made a mistake or done something wrong to harm or hurt someone.

One example could be that I am an usher and I treat everybody the same. However, if you treat everyone harshly and abruptly that does not make your behavior correct. If you do not know what love behavior is, you are unaware of the harm you are doing to another individual. It should not be assumed because someone has the Holy Spirit that they instantly know how to treat people.

Some people feel the love of God but do not know how to express it properly. Often, we assume that because they should be convicted by God's Spirit, they will change and not treat people badly. However, history in some churches reveals that there are saints that have been around for twenty years who believe that there is nothing wrong with the way they treat people.

They believe that they are acting in love. Even though they may have acted unkindly to individuals and may have injured someone emotionally and now they don't want to come back to the church. The Bible in **John 12:32** says that no man is drawn to God unless the love of God draws him.

When Jesus gave His life on the cross at Calvary He did it because He loved us. It is this love that draws men to Christ even now. If we are not fully aware of how to reflect the love of God to each other, how can we draw men from the world into the church? Worldliness causes the church to appear similar to the world.

Keep the Bond Of Love

Click-Free-Vector-Images Source

In the world, you can suffer hurt and harm because of bitterness, anger, frustration, confusion, pain, and irritation. The world must teach supervisors, teachers, directors, presidents, etc. how to be sensitive to others or it will be considered discrimination, sexual harassment, and abuse. The church must face the fact that these same people enter the church doors every Sunday.

The church is like that Pool of Bethesda which was full of sick folks. The sickness, in this case, is not physical ailments, but the anguish of bitterness, pain, abuse, and frustration. Every time you enter a church, you see an usher, praise leader, choir member, church member, preacher, and pastor. However, we forget that these individuals are people who may have been wounded by the world.

Sometimes we forget that we are individuals who have come out of the world into the church. You will always be a sinner saved by the grace of God through the shed blood of the Lamb. Remember that it is only Christ's blood that covers our sins. That is the reason our minds must be constantly renewed to keep our minds stayed on Jesus.

It is through Christ that we see ourselves as we are and recognize the faults, inadequacies, and shortcomings in ourselves. Christ demonstrated His love for us and accepted us as we were with our imperfections. We must extend the same to our brethren.

The members of the church must feel accepted and loved by everyone. That is the only way we can convince the world that we are indeed the children of God, the Father.

Central Truth: The Church is full of people who are redeemed from a world that is full of hurt and pain. We must learn to accept and express love to each other so that we can be healed from the heartache of the world.

THE BIBLICAL DESCRIPTION
OF LOVE

John Hain graphic artist

In the church, we have the anointing of God's Spirit to guide us in all decisions. The Bible says "...***be as wise as a serpent and gentle as a dove" (Matthew 10:16)***. How can we be wise as a serpent? The serpent is the world, and the dove is God's Spirit. Therefore, we must know how to use God's Spirit to function in the world. How can the church be different from the world? How can we show Christian love behavior?

The answer is to learn what Christian love behavior is and practice this behavior. The only way this can happen is for us to be humble enough to ask God if we are truly showing this behavior. The Bible has a few ways to tell us if we are showing love behavior and it is in **1 Corinthians chapter 13**. First of all, the Bible teaches in **I Corinthians 13:3** that it does not matter if you are giving money or making a physical sacrifice, without love, these things are worthless.

"And though I bestow all my goods to feed the poor, and though I give my body to be burned, and have not charity, it profiteth me nothing" Therefore, God requires us to behave in love from our hearts. This means that we cannot buy our way in or out of situations with God.

He expects true and honest behavior of love from us. Therefore, He explains to us that love does certain things and has certain characteristics by which it can be identified if it is love that we are reflecting:

Love suffereth long: This means that love does not give up on something or someone quickly because they have not reached your specific expectations.

Love is kind: This means that love shows compassion and concern and does not try to instigate a problem or negative situation between individuals.

Love does not envy: This means that love is not jealous of someone else's success or good fortune.

Love does not vaunteth itself: This means that love does not promote itself and draw attention to the good deeds that are done and does not look for recognition of men/women.

Love does not behave itself unseemly: This means that a person will not create a scene by being loud and hurtful to others.

Love is not puffed up: This means that we will not be egotistical and caught up in our abilities and feeling that we are always right and there is no other way to attack a problem or situation but our way.

Love does not seek its own gain: This means that you do not seek to get your personal gain from situations and when it does not benefit you; you are not willing to help in accomplishing the goals for God

Love is not easily provoked: This means that an individual will not fly off the handle and say and do things that are cruel and mean.

Love does not think evil: This means that when you see someone who is female talking to someone that is male, you do not automatically assume that there must be something funny going on because of your own inappropriate thinking.

Love does not rejoice in iniquity: This means that you do not get happy when you see someone fall into a sinful situation or when you see someone down and out because they are being convicted by God.

Love rejoiceth in the truth: This means that when someone gets the victory, whether it is someone you like or dislike, you can show love and rejoice. In addition, you can rejoice in the Lord for their victory.

Love beareth all things: This means that no matter the situation God requires you to deal with, you will be willing to commit to whatever God wants you to do.

63

Love endureth all things: This means that those things that God asks you to do may not always be glamorous, but you are willing to do them with humility and not feel that it is beneath your abilities because you are better than this particular task.

Love hopeth all things: This means that you will have faith when the pastor asks the church to pray for someone who is in the front of the church and needs everyone to be on one accord for deliverance to take place and you are willing to have hope regardless of what that person did to you that morning.

Love never fails: This means that you will stand for God and His people no matter what the devil afflicts you with. You will guard and protect God's people and His anointing in your life. You will not have too much pride to go tell the pastor or someone else what God has revealed to you about their situation. It also means that you will pray to God before you open your mouth and seek God for counsel before approaching individuals to assure you are being used as a tool of God and not of Satan.

The description outlined above explains how love behavior should be displayed.

The question before us is, how do we show this loving behavior? Remember that in our natural man, we do not have the ability to show the love of God, but after salvation has taken place, we have everything necessary to show this love. If we do not learn how to show love, then instead of deliverance, we will have bondage.

The bondage of anger, meanness, unkindness, resentment, cruelty, and just plain bad behavior. The outcome will be that we will have a church full of wounded and injured individuals instead of victorious joyful individuals. When individuals are in bondage, they cannot perform God's purpose freely.

Central Truth: Christian love behavior is not just what we learn, it is what we must do. It is a lifestyle the Bible has shown us in **1 Corinthians 13**.

THE DEVIL'S INTENTION

Darksouls1 graphic artist

Devil's Attack On The Church

The above chart was created by Arlette Thomas-Fletcher

The devil intends to vex the pastor with bondage and move to the ministers that surround the pastor and branch out to the ushers, choir leaders, etc. until he has gotten to everyone. This allows the devil to build a stronghold in a church and then there is little, or no fruit received. The preceding page is an outline of how the devil attacks the church and structures a stronghold in the church. These are the behaviors that creep in under the leadership or through the congregation which the devil passes around like a virus.

The virus infects the church and it does not stop until everyone is infected. Then you begin to find that the church is becoming dead and carnal.This can be stopped if we put our trust and faith in God, knowing that it is the love of God that destroys the yoke of the enemy. Remember that it is through love that we can gain deliverance. It is the love of God that sent Jesus to the cross to die for all the sins of mankind.

Therefore, it is the love of God that is our refuge and fortress and destroys the barriers of the devil and pulls down all strongholds. Remember that we wrestle not against flesh and blood but against spiritual wickedness in high places. The highest place that the devil wants to reach in the church is the pastor. After he gets the head, the body will follow. Therefore, it is important to prepare for a battle against the enemy before this takes place.

In preparing for this, it is important to recognize that God wants us to be aware of the fact that we already have the tools for victory. Therefore, God has given us weapons for battle before the war takes place. God gave us the weapon through the Holy Ghost when He saved us. We access the weapon we need through prayer and the guidance of the Holy Spirit.

Sometimes training is necessary to help leaders understand how to help the individuals that they meet in church and their everyday life.

Mote Oo graphic artist

Proverbs 22:6 "Train up a child in the way he should go and when he is old these things shall not depart from him"

The importance of training comes from God. The scripture tells us as parents to train up a child in the way he should go and when he is old, these things will not depart from him. What *are* we, if not God's children? As His children, He wants us to be trained in the proper use of His Word in our lives. Jesus tells us that the greatest commandment He ever gave us was to love one another. We must practice Christian love behavior. What is Christian love behavior?

Remember what was outlined in **I Corinthians 13**: that is the love behavior that God expects. The key is how we practice this behavior at all times. The Bible gives us a prescription for every condition like a doctor gives you a prescription for every illness. Therefore, in order to display Christian love behavior, we must first face that our behavior to one another needs great improvement.

The first step is the confession of the sin of not showing God's love to His people in the way He would have us to convey His love and affection. The Bible says that *"If we confess our sins, He is faithful and just to forgive us of our sins, and to clean us from all unrighteousness."* The second step is our profession of what we believe based on the Word of God. We have to believe that God's plan for love behavior is the right plan.

Therefore, if we are prideful and think that we are showing the love of God, or that people need to grow up, are whining, or immature, that is not God's point to us because what are we, if not some of those things at times to God? God wants us to pray and look beyond the faults of man and see their need as God does for us.

However, God never said this would be an easy quest. Therefore, outlined in the following pages, is a training plan which is taken from the Word of God. The foundation for this plan can be found in some of these chapters in the Bible: I Corinthians 13, Romans 8: 5-11, James 3:1-18 and James 4. Other scriptures to research for further clarification would be:

Ephesians 4-6

Phillippians 1-4

Colossians 4

I Thessalonians 1

II Thessalonians 1-3

I Timothy 3-6

II Timothy 1-4

Titus 1-3

Hebrew10-13

James 1:13-15-5, 22-25, 26-27

Central Truth: The devil intends to infect the church with negative and sinful habits that inhibit the manifestations of the power of God. We must be trained in the proper use of God's words to ensure that Christian love behavior rules and pulls down all the strongholds of the devil.

SEVEN STEPS ON HOW LOVE BEHAVIOR CAN BE TRAINED IN THE CHURCH

Joseph Mucira

Every training plan should have learning objectives and the objective of the plan is to train leaders and church members in Christian love behavior. The first step should be to outline the love behaviors which are reflected in **I Corinthians 13**. Then develop a poster and display it with the behaviors outlined in the church building. It should be placed in plain view of the parishioners.

It is imperative that new members are taught love behavior in the church. Make sure people that are being trained for leadership understand the church expects them to show God's love behavior to all individuals. Make sure that each leader understands what Christian love behavior is and how to display it. Offer counsel to all leaders and church members if they feel that they have been injured or wounded by someone in leadership or membership.

Counsel leaders on the proper spiritual techniques to use to assure that love behavior is being shown to everyone. It is very important to recognize that all of God's people are important. As believers, our role is to assure that everyone is respected and treated in a manner that shows the love of God. This should be instilled by finding ways to address Christian love behavior in every sermon.

It does not mean that all sermons are about love behavior, it just means that there should be an intentional effort to include this topic in sermons when God leads the pastor to speak on it in his/her sermon.

STEP I- Every member and leader should be able to have an overview of what Christian love behavior is and how to display it in the church and their everyday lives. Develop a plan that should be used to outline what Christian love behavior is by using the model that is in "The Biblical Description of Love" chapter. Begin the class by going around the room and asking each person what this plan is and what it means to them.

STEP II- After each person has explained what God's Christian love behavior plan is and what it means to them, give them a copy of the plan which is outlined above and incorporate what should be placed in the definition as the Holy Spirit guides you. A handout with Further explanation of love behavior can be found in **I Corinthians 13.** To help individuals understand how this applies to their everyday lives, each section should be explained with an example. It is also a good way to give all individuals an understanding of what God's love behavior is and how He expects it to be displayed.

Love endureth all things. This means that those things that God asks you to do may not always be glamorous but you are willing to do them with humility: you don't feel that it is beneath your abilities to take on any job or task because you are better than this particular assignment.

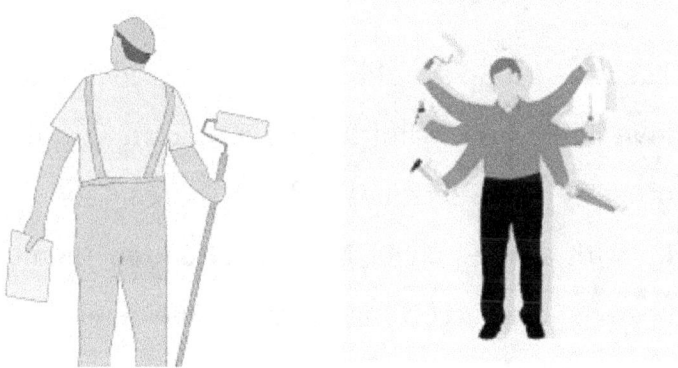

Mohamed Ashan graphic artist

STEP III ACTIVITY:

A role-play activity is a good way to demonstrate the importance of love behavior. The person who is instructing the leaders or members in the training class should request that everyone get a partner for a role-play activity. Each person should be required to think of a time that someone injured or wounded him or her.

Then they should tell the other person what kind of situation they want to act out based on the experience they have had in their life. This role-play needs to be as real-life as possible to get the effect of the exercise across to the class and the participants. After each team has developed their role-play, they should perform it briefly before the group.

Then the group should determine, based on the list of love behaviors, whether the situation was handled properly by the persons involved. The team should come up with a role-play of how the situation should have been handled according to the outline of love behavior in **I Corinthians 13**.

STEP IV CHURCH SURVEY:

Another exercise that can be used is a survey. The survey should be anonymous to get the best response. It should be given to the congregation and leaders and all papers should be put in a locked box on a table at the back of the church.

> *John 14:1 "Let not your heart be troubled: ye believe in God, believe also in me"*

Josep   Monter   Martinez

The survey should be outlined as reflected below with a list of questions that relate to situations of hurt. Below are some sample questions that can be used as a survey instrument:

ANONYMOUS TRUTH SURVEY

1. Have your feelings ever been hurt?

2. Have you ever reacted angrily in response to someone who has hurt your feelings?

3. Have you ever purposely sought revenge on a person because they hurt you or some else feelings?

4. Do you yell and scream at people when you are hurt?

5. Do you feel out of place or like you don't belong when you are around certain people?

6. Would you like to talk to someone about how you feel?

7. Do you know and understand that God has a love behavior?

8. Do you believe you show God's love behavior in your life?

9. When people hurt you in the church do you come back the next Sunday?

10. When people hurt you do you tell someone about it, or do you go home angry?

11. If you could tell someone and resolve what you feel, would you?

12. Do you believe anyone cares about hurt feelings in the church?

13. Have you ever had your feelings severely hurt by leaders in the church?

14. Have you ever had your feelings severely hurt by a church member in church?

The survey method can be used in many ways. To determine whether hurting people is a widespread problem in a church, a pastor can survey the whole congregation. In addition, they can include it in training classes and survey the participants. Either way, it is a good tool to determine the percentage of people that are being hurt and how they feel about the environment that they are in.

After a church survey, the pastor and leaders should review the survey and pray for guidance on how to improve love behavior in their church. They should develop a plan to discourage individuals from arbitrarily hurting people. It should be made clear to all leaders and members that Christian love behavior is a strong foundation in the church and that the church believes in this behavior.

Therefore, injuring individuals should not happen in the church. The devil cannot build a stronghold of hurt and pain if it is not tolerated. This does not mean things will not still happen, but it does mean that a high percentage will stop. It also means that if someone gets hurt, it can quickly be attended to and resolved.

STEP V

Make sure that leaders and members understand that love behavior can only be developed if you are living a truly Christian life; outline what living a true Christian life means. A good way to help them determine the meaning is through small group questioning and discussion. Ask the leaders that are in the training to get together in separate groups and discuss what Christian living means to each one of them.

Help leaders to understand that no one can live a Christian life on their own power. **Galatian 3:3 "Are you so foolish? Having begun by the Spirit, are you now being perfected by the flesh?"** Leaders need to understand that no one can live a Christian life without the guidance and understanding that God gives them through the Holy Spirit.

Therefore, we must all ask God to fill and renew us in His spirit each day of our lives. It is His power that we access through the Holy Spirit which gives us the anointing to live a Christian life. Christ empowers us daily to grow in his grace and be the children of God he expects us to be. For leaders to be effective, they must share their own experiences of Christian living.

This will allow them to understand how problems may affect members of the church body. Each person faces difficulties in their daily lives such as anger, frustration, resentment, disappointment, misunderstanding, and feelings of displacement. Therefore, it would be imperative to set up a mock church situation that involves difficult circumstances, such as a problem that may occur in spiritual living.

Then, have them demonstrate what could be done to resolve this situation. Have them set up a time when they will get together and participate as a team in discussing the issues of Christian living. Next, each group presents a full report that summarizes the lessons of the group exercise. Each group member should actively participate and have a part to contribute to the team/ group presentation.

Now have an open discussion in the seminar as to what else may be involved in their testimonies of Christian living. Finally, conduct an exercise using the questions and scripture outlined below to analyze and access how they feel about what has been learned and the effect it will have on their future life.

1. How does the scripture and statement below relate to your life?

Romans 8:5-11

> *"For they that are after the flesh do mind the things of the flesh; but they that are after the Spirit the things of the Spirit."*

Following the flesh keeps you in a worldly situation.

2. Do you believe that you are living a carnal life?

Romans 8:6

> *6 "For to be carnally minded is death; but to be spiritually minded is life and peace."*

Having a carnal mind separates us from the Spirit.

3. Do you know the difference between a carnal mind and a spiritual mind?

Romans 8:7

> *7 "Because the carnal mind is enmity against God; for it is not subject to the law of God, neither indeed can be."*

A carnal mind is worldly, and worldliness separates our mind from God.

4. What is the difference between living a spiritual life and a worldly life?

Romans 8:8

> **8 "So then they that are in the flesh cannot please God."**

If we follow the world, we are not following God.

5. What does being a new creature in Christ mean to you?

Romans 8:9

> **9 "But ye are not in the flesh, but in the Spirit, if so be that the Spirit of God dwell in you. Now if any man have not the Spirit of Christ, he is none of his."**

You are a new creature that God has saved, so you should not be living according to your old life.

6. What does it mean for the old man to die?

Romans 8:10

> **10 "And if Christ be in you, the body is dead because of sin; but the Spirit is life because of righteousness."**

If you accepted Christ into your life, then your old man is dying, let it go so that the new man can emerge.

7. How do you believe God's spirit works inside of you?

Romans 8:11

11 "But if the Spirit of him that raised up Jesus from the dead dwell in you, he that raised up Christ from the dead shall also quicken your mortal bodies by his Spirit that dwelleth in you"

It is essential that you understand that God's Holy Spirit lives inside you. If you need help living a Christian life and showing love behavior, God will provide it for you. Let Him know your needs through prayer.

STEP VI

THE IMPORTANCE OF TRUTH AND COMPASSIONATE HUMBLE ACTION

Present a story from the Bible that reflects the truth, action, and compassion of Jesus. Some examples could be the story of Saul and David, the story of David and Absalom, or the story of David and Uriah. Cain and Abel would be another story to look at and the story of John the Baptist and Salome's revenge for requesting his head.

Present the question: **"do you think that these people could have been wounded and bitter people**?" Then let the leaders read the scripture in **James chapters 3 and 4** in its entirety.

Make sure you bring in different versions of the scripture, for example, the New American Standard Version and the Amplified Bible version. This will give different perspectives and a clearer understanding of the Bible terminology.

Gerd Altmann

STEP VII

CONCLUSION AND REVIEW

Go back over the objective of the training which is to promote Christian love behavior and to stop people from being wounded in the church. Explain that the church is a refuge and that people should expect to come into the church and find sanctuary. Explain the importance of teaching Christian love behavior because it is the greatest commandment that Jesus gave to the church.

Also, it might benefit your leaders to take a beginner's course in Counseling to help them focus on abused and emotionally injured individuals. Loyola College in Maryland has a good Pastoral Counseling program, they may offer some courses from that program that would expand the knowledge base of the leaders who are working with wounded individuals.

There are many colleges offering Pastoral Counseling programs online, as well as in your geographic area. Please do the research to find these classes to use as a resource for your leaders. Make sure that you close the class with a prayer that focuses on the objective of the class. Explain that love behavior is damaged by bad actions through wicked attitudes and negative communication that come out of another person's mouth.

We must pray before we speak to individuals about sensitive situations. Make sure all leaders understand why Jesus fasted forty days and forty nights and why the children of Israel were in the wilderness for forty years. **Luke 4:1-2,** after Jesus was baptized by John the Baptist, he fasted for forty days and nights to prepare Himself to do God's will in His ministry to the people.

87

Throughout the Bible, fasting was used when seeking the guidance of God. **Ezra 8:21-23** teaches us that the people fasted as they journeyed to Jerusalem to show God that they totally or wholly trusted in Him for help. No one is required to fast. Fasting is a choice that a Christian should make on his or her own. Fasting has been used to control our physical pleasure and desires.

It is because it enhances our spirit and makes it stronger. This is done by feasting on the Word of God and allowing the Holy Spirit to feed us with spiritual food. The children of Israel were required to fast to draw them closer to God. It was to help them let go of their dependence on flesh and to encourage them to lean on the Lord. During the time of fasting, it is also a time for repentance over past sins.

When we fast, we allow God's spirit to be the leader and our flesh to become more subservient to the Holy Spirit. Make sure they understand the importance of purging the old man and how fasting and praying keep the flesh subject to the spirit. Develop the system of a monthly meeting to discuss issues in the church. The discussion should be focused on how to help wounded individuals.

Teach leaders that fasting and praying as a group can help them gain God's revelation regarding the different ways to assist with helping wounded individuals through the word of God.

Central Truth: Learning and showing Christian love behavior is every member's duty. Everyone in the church must be committed to it. It is not the responsibility of the leaders alone, It is the mission of the whole church.

Journal Notes:

_____

_____

_____

_____

_____

_____

_____

_____

_____

Journal Notes:

_____

_____

_____

_____

_____

_____

_____

_____

_____

_____

Journal Notes:

_____

_____

_____

_____

_____

_____

_____

_____

_____

_____

Journal Notes:

References:

Merriam-Webster dictionary definition of Love.

All Bible Scripture from the King James Version and the New King James Version of the Bible throughout the book.

Other Books By The Author

https://arlettethomasfletcher.com

www.ingramcontent.com/pod-product-compliance
Lightning Source LLC
Chambersburg PA
CBHW060355180626
46817CB00008B/3022